MW00787888

BETTER TOGETHER: ANIMAL GROUPS
ORCA WHALE
PODS

by Karen Latchana Kenney

pogo

Ideas for Parents and Teachers

Pogo Books let children practice reading informational text while introducing them to nonfiction features such as headings, labels, sidebars, maps, and diagrams, as well as a table of contents, glossary, and index.

Carefully leveled text with a strong photo match offers early fluent readers the support they need to succeed.

Before Reading

- "Walk" through the book and point out the various nonfiction features. Ask the student what purpose each feature serves.
- Look at the glossary together. Read and discuss the words.

Read the Book

- Have the child read the book independently.
- Invite him or her to list questions that arise from reading.

After Reading

- Discuss the child's questions. Talk about how he or she might find answers to those questions.
- Prompt the child to think more. Ask: Orca whales are apex predators. Do you know any other animals that are apex predators?

Pogo Books are published by Jump!
5357 Penn Avenue South
Minneapolis, MN 55419
www.jumplibrary.com

Library of Congress Cataloging-in-Publication Data

Names: Kenney, Karen Latchana, author.
Title: Orca whale pods / by Karen Latchana Kenney.
Description: Pogo books edition.
Minneapolis, MN: Jump!, Inc., [2020]
Series: Better together: animal groups
Includes index. | Audience: Age 7-10.
Identifiers: LCCN 2019001742 (print)
LCCN 2019002713 (ebook)
ISBN 9781641288569 (ebook)
ISBN 9781641288552 (hardcover : alk. paper)
Subjects: LCSH: Killer whale—Behavior—Juvenile literature.
Social behavior in animals—Juvenile literature.
Classification: LCC QL737.C432 (ebook)
LCC QL737.C432 K47 2020 (print)
DDC 599.53/6—dc23
LC record available at https://lccn.loc.gov/2019001742

Editor: Jenna Trnka
Designer: Jenna Casura

Photo Credits: Tory Kallman/Shutterstock, cover, 3, 23; Lazareva/iStock, 1; Johnny Johnson/Getty, 4; Rebecca Yale/Getty, 5; SuperStock, 6-7; Gerard Lacz/Age Fotostock, 8-9; mauritius images GmbH/Alamy, 10; Sue Clark/Alamy, 11; Rasmus-Raahauge/iStock, 12-13; National Geographic Image Collection/Alamy, 14-15; Gerard Lacz Images/SuperStock, 16; Arco Images GmbH/Alamy, 17; Hugh Harrop/Alamy, 18-19; David Day/Age Fotostock, 20-21.

Printed in the United States of America at Corporate Graphics in North Mankato, Minnesota.

TABLE OF CONTENTS

CHAPTER 1
Pod Talk 4

CHAPTER 2
Mighty Killers 10

CHAPTER 3
Orca Families 16

ACTIVITIES & TOOLS
Try This! 22
Glossary 23
Index 24
To Learn More 24

CHAPTER 1

POD TALK

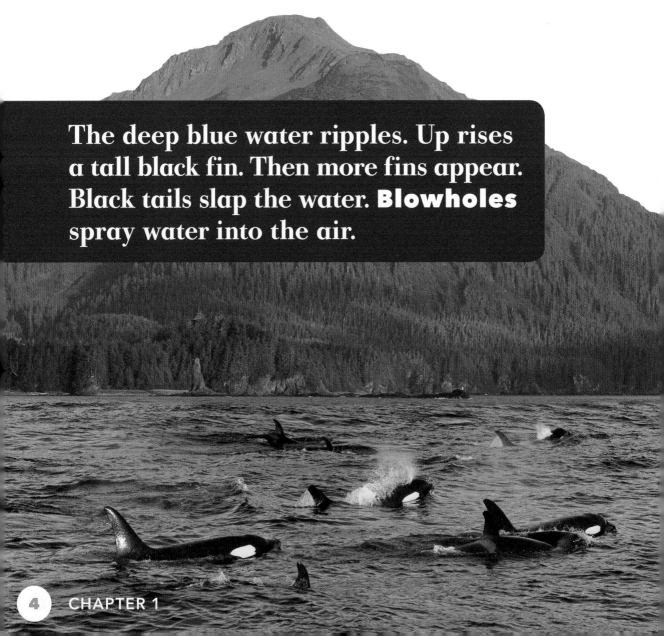

The deep blue water ripples. Up rises a tall black fin. Then more fins appear. Black tails slap the water. **Blowholes** spray water into the air.

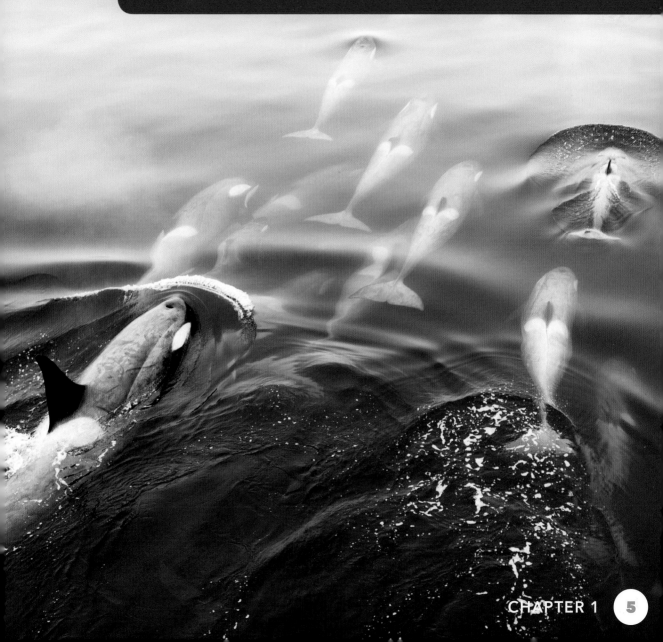

These orca whales are on the move. Their group is called a **pod**. Orca pods live, travel, and hunt together. Pod life helps them survive.

Some pods have up to 40 orcas! The members stay together most of the time. They are very close. The leader of the pod is the oldest mother. The group follows her. She helps them stay together.

TAKE A LOOK!

Orcas have a very distinct color pattern. What are their body parts called? Take a look!

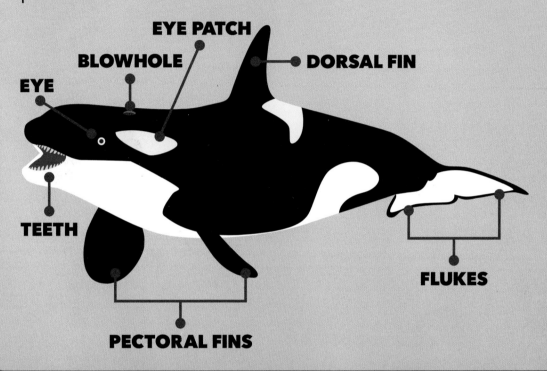

EYE PATCH

BLOWHOLE

DORSAL FIN

EYE

TEETH

PECTORAL FINS

FLUKES

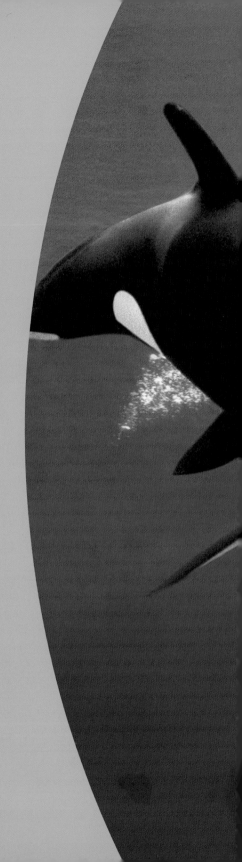

Orcas click, pop, and whistle. They make these sounds by moving air in their blowholes. Sometimes bubbles come out, too.

The sounds bounce off one another. This is called **echolocation**. This is how they **communicate**. This is also how they find **prey** and find their way in dark water.

DID YOU KNOW?

Each orca pod has its own language. No two pods communicate with the same sounds.

CHAPTER 2
MIGHTY KILLERS

Orcas are fierce **predators**. This is why they are also called killer whales. But they are actually a kind of dolphin. Sharp teeth help them eat prey.

seal

Pods work together to hunt prey. This pod in Antarctica finds a seal. The orcas surround it. They swim fast to make a wave. The wave will then push the seal off the ice.

Some pods hunt fish **schools**. How? The orcas **herd** the fish. They blow air bubbles. This makes walls around the school. The fish form a tight ball. Then the orcas slap them with their tails. The fish fall and are easy to eat.

school of fish

TAKE A LOOK!

Take a look at this ocean **food chain**. Krill are at the bottom. Cod and penguins eat krill. What eats them? Orcas are at the top. They are **apex predators**. Nothing hunts them.

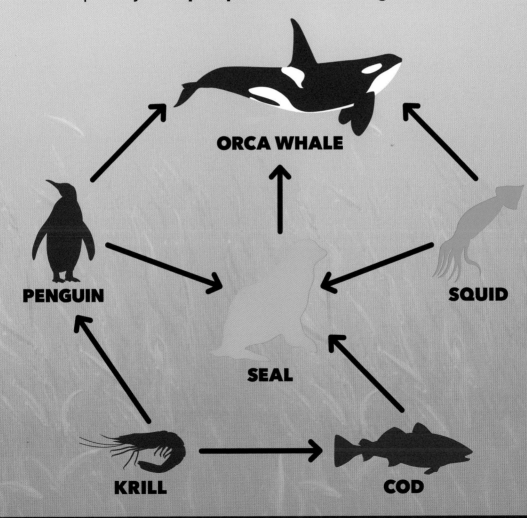

ORCA WHALE

PENGUIN

SQUID

SEAL

KRILL

COD

Pods can also attack animals on land! In Argentina, orcas go onto the beach. They snatch seals and sea lions. Then they twist and turn their bodies. They slide back into the water. Older orcas teach younger ones in the pod. They learn how to hunt this way.

CHAPTER 3

....

ORCA FAMILIES

The pod grows when baby orcas are born. Orca whale babies are called calves.

calf

nursing

Each calf is bigger than a person. It needs its mother to survive. Mothers keep their calves close. They **nurse** them. They form a close **bond**.

The young orcas have a lot to learn. Older orcas teach calves how to hunt. The calves learn how to catch prey.

Hunting is hard work. Luckily, younger orcas have many teachers in the pod. They stay together for many years. Together, orcas rule the ocean.

DID YOU KNOW?

Orcas live a long time in their pods. They can live to be 80 years old!

ACTIVITIES & TOOLS

ORCA HUNT

Orcas hunt together. They gather large schools of fish in a big ball. Try gathering balloons, just like orcas.

What You Need:
- 20 balloons
- garbage bag
- stopwatch or timer
- pencil and paper
- two friends

❶ Gather two friends together. Blow up all 20 balloons. Put them in the garbage bag.

❷ Ask one friend to throw all of the balloons up into the air. Try to gather them into the garbage bag as fast as you can. Have the other friend time you. Record how long it took.

❸ Try gathering the balloons with both friends. See how fast the three of you can do it. Time yourselves and record the time it took.

❹ Next, make a plan with your friends. See if you can gather the balloons faster than before. For example, one person could hold the garbage bag, while the other two gather balloons.

❺ Test a few plans to see what works best. What is your fastest time? Which plan worked the best?

apex predators: Predators at the top of a food chain that are not hunted by any other animal.

blowholes: Nostrils on the top of whale and dolphin heads that are used for breathing.

bond: A close connection or strong feelings toward one another.

communicate: To share information or feelings through sounds and gestures.

echolocation: Locating objects by reflected sound.

food chain: An ordered arrangement of animals and plants in which each feeds on the one below it in the chain.

herd: To move animals together in a group.

nurse: To feed babies milk.

pod: A group of orca whales.

predators: Animals that hunt other animals for food.

prey: Animals that are hunted by other animals for food.

schools: Tight groups of fish that swim and feed together.

INDEX

apex predators 13

blowholes 4, 7, 8

body parts 7

bond 17

bubbles 8, 12

calves 16, 17, 19

communicate 8

echolocation 8

fish schools 12

food chain 13

hunt 5, 11, 12, 13, 14, 19, 20

ice 11

killer whales 10

land 14

leader 6

mother 6, 17

nurse 17

pattern 7

prey 8, 10, 11, 19

seal 11, 13, 14

sea lions 14

sounds 8

teach 14, 19, 20

teeth 7, 10

travel 5

wave 11

TO LEARN MORE

Finding more information is as easy as 1, 2, 3.

1 Go to www.factsurfer.com

2 Enter "orcawhalepods" into the search box.

3 Choose your book to see a list of websites.

FACT SURFER